Larry Gets Lost in the Library

Illustrated by John Skewes
Written by Eric Ode

Larry Gets Lost series created by John Skewes

little bigfoot

an imprint of sasquatch books
seattle, wa

For Mike Calkins, friend and inspiration.

As always, I hope you like it. —JS

With heartfelt appreciation to librarians everywhere. —EO

Manufactured in China by C&C Offset Printing Co. Ltd. Shenzhen, Guangdong Province, in April 2021

LITTLE BIGFOOT with colophon is a registered trademark of Penguin Random House LLC

25 24 23 22 21   9 8 7 6 5 4 3 2 1

Editor: Christy Cox
Design: Mint Design

Library of Congress Cataloging-in-Publication Data is available

ISBN: 978-1-63217-324-9 (hardcover)
ISBN: 978-1-63217-413-0 (paperback)

Sasquatch Books
1904 Third Avenue, Suite 710
Seattle, WA 98101

SasquatchBooks.com

This is **Larry**.

This is **Pete**.

They're here on the farm.
What a wonderful treat!

With critters to care for
and work to be done,
a summer at Grandma's
is loaded with fun.

Now Larry hears honking.
What's this all about?
"It's bookmobile day!"
Grandma says with a shout.

They watch the doors open.
Then Pete clambers up.
But Larry must wait.
It's no place for a pup.

Soon Pete reappears
holding books 1, 2, 3.
He sits down to read
with his back to a tree.

But Larry thinks sadly,
There's no book for me.

He runs to the truck,
and he hops in the back.
If he can't have a book,
then he might find a snack.

But then, with a click,
and as quick as a bark,
poor Larry has found
he's alone in the dark.

The truck engine rumbles.
That pup's in a bind.
He's on an adventure
with Pete far behind.

He peeks through a curtain
and nothing looks right.
No farmhouse. No horses.
And no Pete in sight.

They've come to a town,
and wherever he looks,
Larry sees buildings
and people with books.

They come to a stop,
and the doors open wide.
That building's so busy!
Could Pete be inside?

As rain starts to fall
from a dark, heavy cloud,
Larry runs past the driver.
He slips through a crowd.
But then—what a problem.
No dogs are allowed!

That pup's cold and tired.
He's worried and wet.
But soon Larry thinks
he might get inside yet.

He squishes

and squeezes,

then, *plop*,
reappears

in a box filled with books
from his paws to his ears.

Larry climbs to the top,
and then what does he see?
A room full of folks
working hard as can be.

One man's fixing books
that are falling apart.
One woman stacks books
on a big, sturdy cart.

And each is too busy
with jobs to complete
to notice a pup
who's out searching for Pete.

He crawls on a shelf.
It's a good place to hide.
But soon Larry finds
he is off on a ride.

He bumps through a door,
and then—what a surprise!
Walls filled with books—
every color and size!

Big books and little books.
Red, green, and blue ones.
Bright, fancy picture books.
Old books and new ones!

People on sofas,
on chairs, and on rugs.

595.7
INSECTS

A boy learning how
to bake cookies and cakes.

Larry hurries upstairs
and finds shiny machines.

A small, quiet corner
with new magazines.

A dark, crowded room
filled with bright, flashing screens.

What's this? Larry wonders
while snooping along.
A room full of children.
They're singing a song.

"Now, time for a story!"
the children are told.
"Go choose a stuffed animal.
Something to hold."

One girl looks around
for a toy she can cuddle.
"This puppy dog's real,
and he's wet as a puddle!"

The bookmobile driver
comes running inside.
"So here's where my buddy
decided to hide.

"Let's get you back home.
This has been quite a day!"

They hop in the truck,
and they're soon on their way.

The animals cheer
with a moo, neigh, and quack.
"It's Larry!" shouts Pete.
"We're so glad that you're back!"

They hug and they dance
as the critters look on.
Then Pete quickly disappears.
Where has he gone?

Soon he returns.
But now, what does he carry?

A book that's just right
for his best buddy, Larry.